BACKSTABBED

BY AGENT 111

DURVISH DARYANI

Copyright © Durvish Daryani
All Rights Reserved.

This book has been published with all efforts taken to make the material error-free after the consent of the author. However, the author and the publisher do not assume and hereby disclaim any liability to any party for any loss, damage, or disruption caused by errors or omissions, whether such errors or omissions result from negligence, accident, or any other cause.

While every effort has been made to avoid any mistake or omission, this publication is being sold on the condition and understanding that neither the author nor the publishers or printers would be liable in any manner to any person by reason of any mistake or omission in this publication or for any action taken or omitted to be taken or advice rendered or accepted on the basis of this work. For any defect in printing or binding the publishers will be liable only to replace the defective copy by another copy of this work then available.

Contents

Preface

So, this book is basically about a person who was betrayed by his own friend. To know what happened to the betrayer, read the book.

Enjoy!

Acknowledgements

I Would like to thank my mother and my father, who let me pursue my passion. A special thanks goes to Nitya Jitesh Patel and Rishit Moryani, both my closest friends, for reviewing my book, and helped me in many a way.

Investigations

Agent 111 and Agent 607 come to know about some sad news and a burglary. They start investigating on the case. Read the book to know what happens next.

Enjoy!

CHAPTER ONE

TWO PIECES OF BAD NEWS AT THE SAME TIME

It was a sunny day. Kevin (Agent 111) and Kimmy (Agent 607) had just been engaged. Kevin shouted "Honey, John Yamamoto (A Cop) is calling me. "

"Answer it, it might be urgent." Kimmy replied. Kevin did as told. John was about to give them sad news. In fact, very very very sad news. John said, "Kevin, I'm sad to be the messenger of this news. Barberra Kyne (A Cop) may not exist any more. "

" Tell this to Kimmy." said Kevin, who was trying to control his emotions. Kimmy broke down as soon as she heard the news. She now called Juliet Johnson, and gave her the news. Juliet also reacted to the news the same way Kimmy did.

Meanwhile, sitting on the couch, Kevin was thinking, " What a great friend Kyne was. What a pity she is no more." He was struggling to stop the tears that were threatning to burst out, but he succeeded. Meanwhile, John called him again, "Her cremation is tommorow, at 9:00 in the evening, but you have to solve a case before that.

Some people have looted the house of Sir Whittington. Many priceless things have been stolen. Like a photo of him and his late parents.You'll have to solve this case before Kyne is Cremated. I won't be able to help you. It is up to you and Kimmy to solve this case. You have exactly 26 hours to solve this case. "

"OK" Replies Kevin, Hanging up.

CHAPTER TWO

THE BURGLARY

Kevin started his Lamborghini. Kimmy sat in and they drove to Sir Whittington's mansion. On the way, Kevin told Kimmy. "Don't call me by name there, instead by code name. I will do the same."

"OK" Pat came the reply. They reached Whittington's mansion. The political leader himself came to recieve them. "Ah, there you are. I still do not know your names. " Said Whittington. Kevin replied, " I'm Kevin, and this is my fiance, Kimmy."

"Keaton? Kevin Keaton?" Asked Whiitington. Kevin nodded. "Don't you remember me? I'm Whiitington Blake, your former classmate." Said Blake. Kevin replied " It's you? Oh! I cant help but to think that my old friend is a politician, on the rank of the Vice-President, where it is also very difficult for the hollywood stars to reach. Tell me, when did the burglary take place?"

"Yesterday" Came the reply. Kevin removed his extra-expensive microscope and began scanning the ground for tracks of the burglars. The tracks led towards the heart of the city, Grand Conventional Hall. Kevin and Kimmy followed the tracks, which led to the center of the hall. All of a sudden, the tracks ceased to continue. Agent 111 asked

Agent 607, " Scan the surroundings, to find a-"

" Look up, the glass roof is shattered open. The burglars might have escaped from there."Agent 607 interrupted. By the time the agents reached the terrace, the burglars had escaped. But still, a faint noise of the copter's blades was heard. Agent 111 removed his spare phone, turned on location and threw it to the area where the chopper was heard.

The phone fell inside the chopper. Agent 111 and Agent 607 could now track the chopper. The copter landed in New Jersey and the burglars ran away. The agents arrived in New Jersey and chased after the burglars. The Agents removed their microscopes and followed the tracks. The far they went, the tracks turned paler. It was turning hard to track.

Suddenly, the tracks dissapeared, leaving no sign of the burglars. They scanned their surroundings for any clues. Agent 607 spotted a grappling hook stuck on a building quarter a kilometre away. Agent 111 looked at Agent 607. Yes, she was thinking what he was thinking. The grappling hook was exactly what the Agents needed.

The Truth Revealed

I hope you liked the book so far. Inhere, the real criminal behind the burglary gets exposed. Do you want to know who it is? Read ahead to know.

Enjoy!

CHAPTER THREE

BACKSTABBED

As soon as the Agents saw the hook, they ran towards the building. But, the way to the building was full of obstacles, Claymore bombs, grenades, logs of wood and what not? It took them an hour to go past those.

First, the Claymore bombs. Agent 111 shot a bullet each at them. The bombs burst, and hundreds of nails came out. They removed them out with a broomstick.

Then came the grenades. 'BOOM'! 'BOOM'! 'BOOM'!. This place was a wreck within minutes. But, luck was not in store for them at that moment.

There were strong, unmovable wood walls, about 50 feet high. Agent 607 sat thinking. Agent 111 shot a bullet at the wall and found out that the wall was very weak. The super strong wood design was only for deception. Then cheering up the disheartened Agent 607, he motioned for her to follow him.

Both of them ran towards the building. Agent 111 looked at his watch. He had three hours left. The agents removed the grappling hook carefully from the rooftop. They went to the nearest police station and ran some fingerprint tests. It turned out to be Whittington's fingerprint. "So, Whittington was the mastermind behind the whole burglary", said Agent 607. Agent 111 nodded, in a way to say yes. All the stuff that was burgled was kept in Whittington's secret warehouse, specially made for the burglary. Whittington was arrested and put behind the bars. Moreover, he was removed from the prestigious post of Vice-President.

Happy but Sad

I can guess now, that you are thinking 'why is the heading of this page like this?' The answer is in the next chapter. Want to know? Read ahead.

Enjoy!

CHAPTER FOUR

A WAX CORPSE

Kevin and Kimmy drove back home. After they changed into black clothes, they drove off to the cemetery. There, they saw the corpse of their beloved friend Barberra. Her body was shining as if oil was put on her from days.

Kevin's curiosity reached its peak. He knew that Barberra hated oil. He removed the lid of her coffin and scratched the corpse. His nails got filled with wax. His joy knew no bounds as he realised that Barberra was alive. She came from behind and jumped at him. " We wanteed to solve this case as soon as possible. So we faked my death and did not give you much time to solve the case." said Barberra

"Sushi?" asked John. Kevin nodded in a way to say yes. On the way to the restaurant, said that he lost a good friend, Kevin messaged Whittington " I would never had thought that you would betray me in a way like this."

About The Author

Durvish is a passionate writer and musician, at a very young age. Born in 2011, he was inspired by many of the famous writers such as Elissabetta Dami, who is the author of Geronimo Stilton and Jeff Kinney who is the author of The Wimpy Kid Series. His previous works comprise of Agent 111 The First Mission, published in February 2022.

Social Media:-

Instagram: www.instagram.com/durvish1967/

Chat with me on: daryani.durvish10@gmail.com

Books In The Series

1. Agent 111 The First Mission
2. Backstabbed by Agent 111